This Ladybird Book belongs to:

Published by Penguin Books India
11 Community Centre, Panchsheel Park, New Delhi 110017

3 5 7 9 10 8 6 4

ISBN 978-1-84422-743-3

Printed in Manipal Press Ltd., Manipal

FAVOURITE TALES

The Grumpy King

This Ladybird retelling by
MEERA UBEROI

illustrated by
SUNANDINI BASU

A long time ago, a very grumpy king called Pingola ruled a small kingdom in the hills.

Pingola was a very good king. He made sure his people had enough to eat and that the laws were fair. He looked after the roads, and the water, and his people's health. He made the kingdom safe from thieves and robbers.

But he was so busy making sure the kingdom was safe, that he forgot how to be cheerful. And he thought all the people in his kingdom should work as hard as he did, and not spend time having fun.

King Pingola made lots of rules.

He made it compulsory that everyone would go to school until they were fifty. Everyone had to go to bed by nine o'clock, and everyone had to wake up at six in the morning and have cold water baths. No one could eat sweets or light fireworks or have a party.

SCHOOL TILL 50 YEARS
401 NO EATING SWEETS
402 BED BY 9 FOR EVERYONE
403 WAKE UP AT 6 EVERY MORNING
404 COMPULSORY COLD WATER BATHS
405 NO PLAYTIME
406 NO LIGHTING
407

King Pingola was always anxious because there was too much work to do, and he was always angry because he never had enough time to do it in.

He would wake up grumpy in the morning and throw his breakfast at the cook. He would yell at his valet when he came to dress him. He would spend all day checking that everyone was at school, and that everyone was eating enough green vegetables.

He would read the report cards of all the people in his kingdom, and make sure that they were all working hard.

EPORT CARD
elling B
tation C

The only cheerful person in the kingdom was Pingola's son, Prince Singola. The prince was good, kind and generous. He often helped people to do their homework and gave them sweets when no one was looking. So, of course, people loved him.

Sometimes the prince tried to tell his father, ‘Father, you need to have fun sometimes. It is not enough to work all the time.’

But Pingola would get angry, and say, ‘You are still young. You do not realize the importance of hard work.’

Every night, when King Pingola went to bed (at nine o'clock sharp), he was troubled and anxious. There were always report cards he had not managed to read or problems with people's homework to worry about.

One night, as the king lay in bed there were bright flashes in the sky outside his window. And the king heard the sounds of cheering in the streets.

The king rushed to the balcony. There were fireworks! And people in their pajamas dancing and singing in the street.

Dancing! Singing! At this hour!

‘What is this?’ grumbled the king. ‘Don’t they know that it is past their bedtime, that they should be in bed?

The king leaned out and yelled, ‘Oi! What has happened? Why are you dancing? Go to bed at once!’

‘Don’t you know?’ said one of the dancing men, who the king was horrified to realize was his prime minister. ‘King Pingola is dead. He never let us have parties, so we are now celebrating.’

'Dead?' said the king, dazed. 'But I am alive!' But no one paid any attention to him.

All through the next day, the city rejoiced like never before. All schools were shut for a week. Everyone decided to have a party.

All the cooks and bakers brought out their hidden recipe books. They read the books madly because they had all forgotten how to make sweets. Then they cooked all night and made three hundred kinds of sweets. Soon, they were giving away sweets at the street corner and everyone had a lollipop or a laddu in his hand.

It made Pingola sad that everyone seemed so happy to have him gone. He heard one little girl say, with a mouthful of cake, ‘King Pingola was a good man, but I never knew what it was like to have fun.’

Her friend said, ‘The poor man! I don’t think he knew how to have fun!’ and then they both ran away, giggling, to get some candyfloss.

‘They don’t miss me,’ King Pingola thought sadly, and he leaned over the balcony to see where they had gone and suddenly, he was falling, falling, falling …

King Pingola fell out of bed with a big thud. 'Oh, it was all a dream,' he said with great relief. He sat on the edge of his bed, and thought for a while.

The next morning, when the king entered his court, all the ministers were worried to see that there was a great frown on his forehead. 'I have many new laws to make today,' he announced in a deep voice. 'Ministers, take them down!'

'Law 421: Nine o'clock is no longer the bedtime. People can go to bed whenever they like.
'Law 422: People do not have to go to school unless they want to once they are sixteen years old.
'Law 423: All sweetshops are open again, and sweetmakers should give free sweets to children ...'

The king stopped because his prime minister had fainted out of shock, and the other ministers were standing with their mouths hanging open. 'What?'

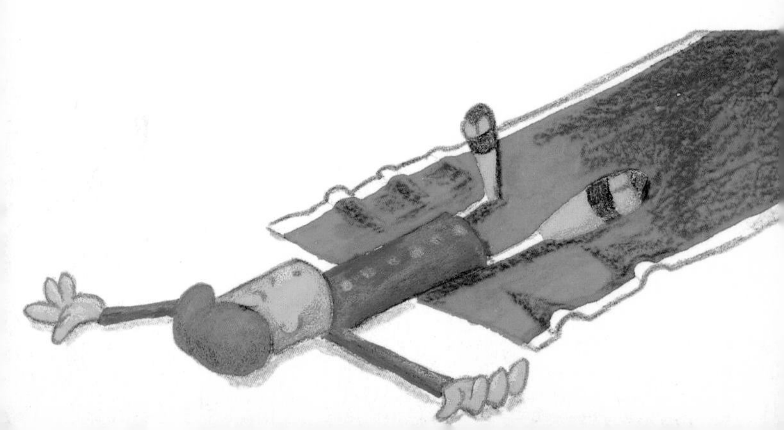

new rules

421 9 o'clock is no longer the bedtime

422 NO SCHOOL after AGE 16

423 ALL sweetshops open

‘But Father,’ said young Prince Singola, ‘what happened? Why are you changing all the laws?’

‘You see, son,’ said the king, with a big smile on his face, ‘I have now realized that it is not enough to work hard. We must also play and have fun.’